CUENTO
DE LUZ

To Manuel and Rosario—my parents—for everything.
To my sister Nati—for everything.
—Fran Nuño

For you, dear bee.
—Zuzanna Celej

STONE
PAPER®
NO TREES - NO WATER - NO BLEACH

This book is printed on **Stone Paper** that is **Silver Cradle to Cradle Certified**®.

Cradle to Cradle™ is one of the most demanding ecological certification systems, awarded to products that have been conceived and designed in an ecologically intelligent way.

Certified
B
Corporation®

Cuento de Luz™ became a **Certified B Corporation** in 2015. The prestigious certification is awarded to companies that use the power of business to solve social and environmental problems and meet higher standards of social and environmental performance, transparency, and accountability.

The Dance of the Bees
Text © 2020 Fran Nuño
Illustrations © 2020 Zuzanna Celej
© 2020 Cuento de Luz SL
Calle Claveles, 10 | Pozuelo de Alarcón | 28223 | Madrid | Spain
www.cuentodeluz.com
Original title in Spanish: *El baile de las abejas*
English translation by Jon Brokenbrow
ISBN: 978-84-18302-27-5
Printed in PRC by Shanghai Cheng Printing Company July 2021, print number 1838-11
2nd printing

FRAN NUÑO

ZUZANNA CELEJ

The Dance
of the
Bees

My grandma loved bees.

She would spend hours and hours just watching them.

One summer, I went along with her on her walks through the countryside,

and she would tell me all about the amazing life of these beautiful insects.

That was when I discovered the dance of the bees.

Every morning, we would leave home
and walk to a different place.
Every day, I learned something new.
"You must know that there are thousands of types of bees," said my grandma.
"Thousands, Grandma?" I said.
"Yes, and some of them don't even sting."

ALONG THE WAY

THE BUZZING OF THE BEES

AND OUR FOOTSTEPS

One day, my grandma asked me a question I didn't know how to answer.

"Do you know why bees are so important for life on our planet?"

"No," I said. "Why are they so important?"

"Because it's thanks to them
that all the fruit grows on the trees," she said.

"Really? And how do they do it?" I asked.
I really wanted to know the answer.

A DAY IN THE COUNTRYSIDE

I WATCH THE BUSY BEES

AS THEY GO TO WORK

We reached a little stream, sat down next to it,

and my grandma answered all my questions.

"The bees land on the flowers to drink the nectar inside them.

Then they take the pollen so they can eat it later on.

But as they buzz along from flower to flower, without realizing it,

they transfer the pollen onto the other flowers.

And it's thanks to them that all the lovely fruit grows."

FROM FLOWER TO FLOWER
BUZZ THE BUSY BEES
MAKING FUTURE FRUITS

We stood in silence for a while, and then I asked her again.

"So, only the bees can do that?"

"No," she said. "Although it's mainly up to them,

there are other insects that do the same thing,

like wasps, butterflies, and flies.

And even other animals like hummingbirds, bats, and rodents.

Oh, of course, the wind also plays its part in the whole process."

I SEE OUR REFLECTIONS

TALKING ABOUT BEES

TOGETHER BY THE STREAM

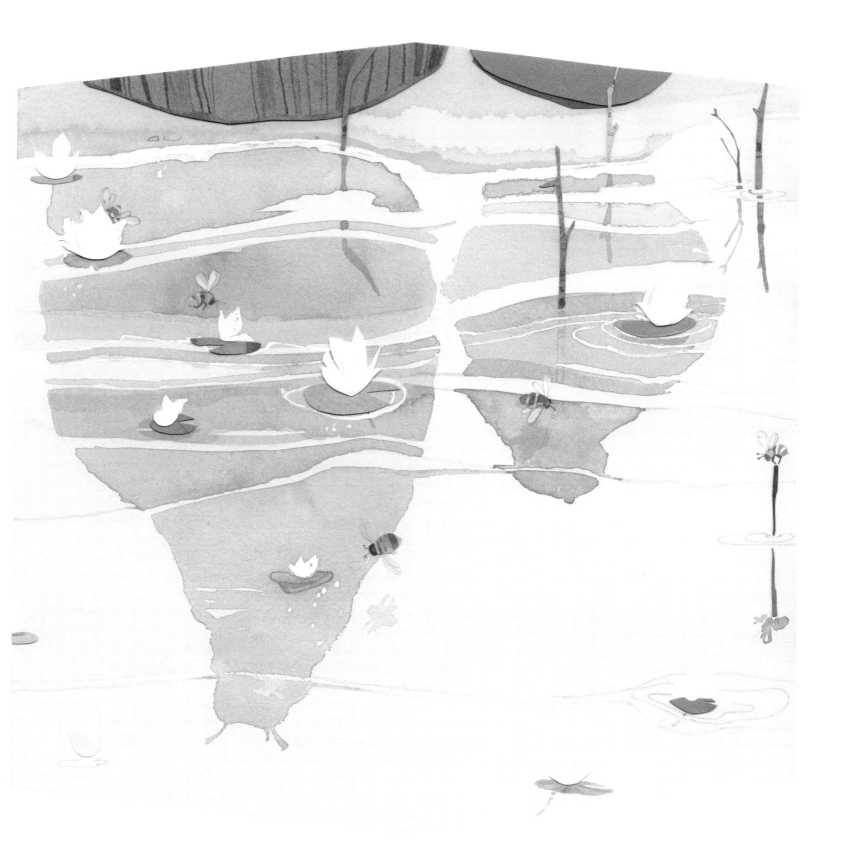

THE BEES ARE SLEEPING

ROCKED TO SLEEP BY THE WIND

ON THE FLOWER

One day, we saw two bees in a flower lying completely motionless.

"Are they dead, Grandma?" I asked, intrigued.

"No, my dear," she said. "They're just asleep. They can't close their eyes,
but when they sleep, their feelers stop moving."

I was amazed when I first saw a beehive

hanging from the branch of a tree.

"Have you never seen one before?" asked my grandma.

"No, I've never seen so many bees together at once," I said.

I couldn't stop staring.

I felt hypnotized by what I was seeing.

AMONG THE GREEN LEAVES

I SEE SOMETHING GOLDEN

A BEEHIVE FULL OF LIFE

My grandma smiled as she watched me and continued with her story.
"They carry the nectar in their tummies and share it with each other,
and then they take it back to the beehive.
Once it's there, some of the bees fan it with their wings
until the nectar gets thicker and thicker.
Finally, they turn it into honey,
which they use to feed their babies."

SO MANY BEES

FLYING AROUND THE BEEHIVE

PROTECTING THE HONEY

The years went by,

and I forgot about that magical summer when I was a little girl.

But one day, I went back to where my grandma's house had once stood.

Nothing of it remained, but my memories came flooding back.

TODAY JUST LIKE THEN I SEE BEES AGAIN ARE THEY THE SAME ONES?

"Look, mommy! What's that bee doing?"

"It's dancing."

"Dancing?"

"That's right. It's showing its friends where the best flowers
are to collect nectar and pollen."

"Let's follow it!"

BUZZING HAPPILY THE BEE KNOWS WELL WHERE THE FLOWERS ARE

We began to follow the bee.

Every now and again, it would hover in the air and do a little dance.

I don't know if I was imagining it or not,

but it was as if it wanted to make sure we knew to follow her.

A TINY MYSTERY

WHERE IS IT TAKING ME?

I FOLLOW A BEE

SIPS A BUSY BEE

ON A CHERRY BLOSSOM

BLACK AND YELLOW STRIPES

Finally, the bee landed on a blossom in a beautiful cherry tree.

Beneath the tree, we found a little pile of stones.

I carefully removed them, one by one.

I didn't know what I would find underneath them,

and my heart began to thump.

I found a small, battered notebook.

"Mommy, open it up. Is there anything written in it?"
On the first page, I saw my grandma's name.

And suddenly, without being able to help myself,
my eyes filled with tears.
I looked up to find the bee that had brought us there,
but it had already left.

BENEATH A TREE

I CAN NO LONGER SEE IT

HAVE YOU GONE LITTLE BEE?

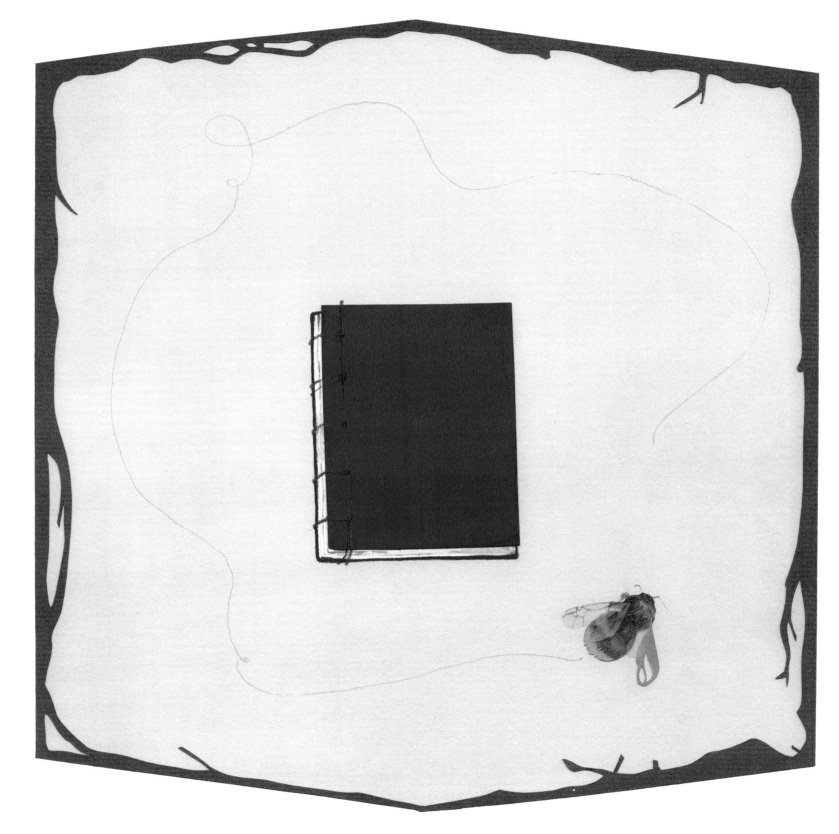

I gave the notebook to my son, and read out loud:

"Dear granddaughter, here are the twelve haikus I wrote

as a reminder of our last summer together.

I never had the chance to give them to you,

but I kept them in a secret place where I was sure

you would find them one day,

thanks to the dance of the bees."

Since then, I have kept these little poems,

the same ones you have read throughout this story,

as if they were my greatest treasure.

Thanks to them, I will never forget everything my grandma taught me

about the wonderful world of the bees.

THE END

About the world of the *haiku*

A *haiku* is a kind of poem that comes from Japan, and dates back to the seventeenth century. It consists of three lines, whose words normally add up to a total of seventeen syllables distributed in a ratio of five-seven-five (in translations of *haikus* from any language to another, this number and ratio usually varies slightly).
In order to be able to write a *haiku*, the *haijin* or *haijina* (the *haiku* poet or poetess) must have previously experienced a revelation. They must have witnessed an event (or taken part in one) that occurred at a specific moment in time, and which in some way or another has moved or driven them to share it with the rest of the world using this type of brief verse. The *haiku* is always written in the present tense, of here and now.

In the *haikus* that have been written strictly following the rules that were set down to regulate their composition in the nineteenth century, we do not find metaphors, similes, or personifications: in other words, the vast majority of the stylistic resources that are normally used in the poetry we know. The subject matter of the *haiku* is assiduously the world of nature, although nowadays many are written that explore themes such as the city. The quality of the *haiku* is further enhanced if its verses give us some type of clue (*kigo*) about the season of the year when the event being described occurred.

When it came to writing this story about the work of the bees, I wanted to use *haikus* (which are also printed vertically, in honor of Japanese script), as I had a large number of revelations running through my mind that featured these beautiful insects. I hope that this book encourages you to continue investigating the wonderful world of the bees, and this way of expressing that which most amazes or surprises us, so that should you wish, you can also start write your own *haikus*.

—Fran Nuño

A BEAUTIFUL STORY WITH HAIKUS